The Great Book Ab

POLAR BEARS

FOR KIDS

To Dudas, my heart
To Teresa, my soul
To Jaime, my rock

The Great Book about Polar Bears ©2021
Text and illustrations by G. Guarita and Qwerty Books.
All rights reserved.
ISBN: 9798530412776

No part of this book can be reproduced or transmitted in any form or by any means without written permission from the publisher.

QWERTY BOOKS

A WORD FROM THE AUTHOR

From polar bears to lizards, from dolphins to dinosaurs, from space to how things work, all that and everything in between, fascinated me growing up.

In different ways, I was blessed with the priceless fortune of growing up in a house full of amazing books. I spent my childhood breathing stories in endless pages with amazing pictures, having fun and learning wonderful and incomparable lessons that I have carried with me throughout my life and passed on to my children and students.

Because I love to teach what I learn, I wrote The Great Book About Polar Bears, so you too can learn, feel and have fun the same way that I learned, felt and had fun growing up surrounded by fascinating books.

So buckle up! It's time to discover The Great Book About Polar Bears for Kids.

G. Guarita

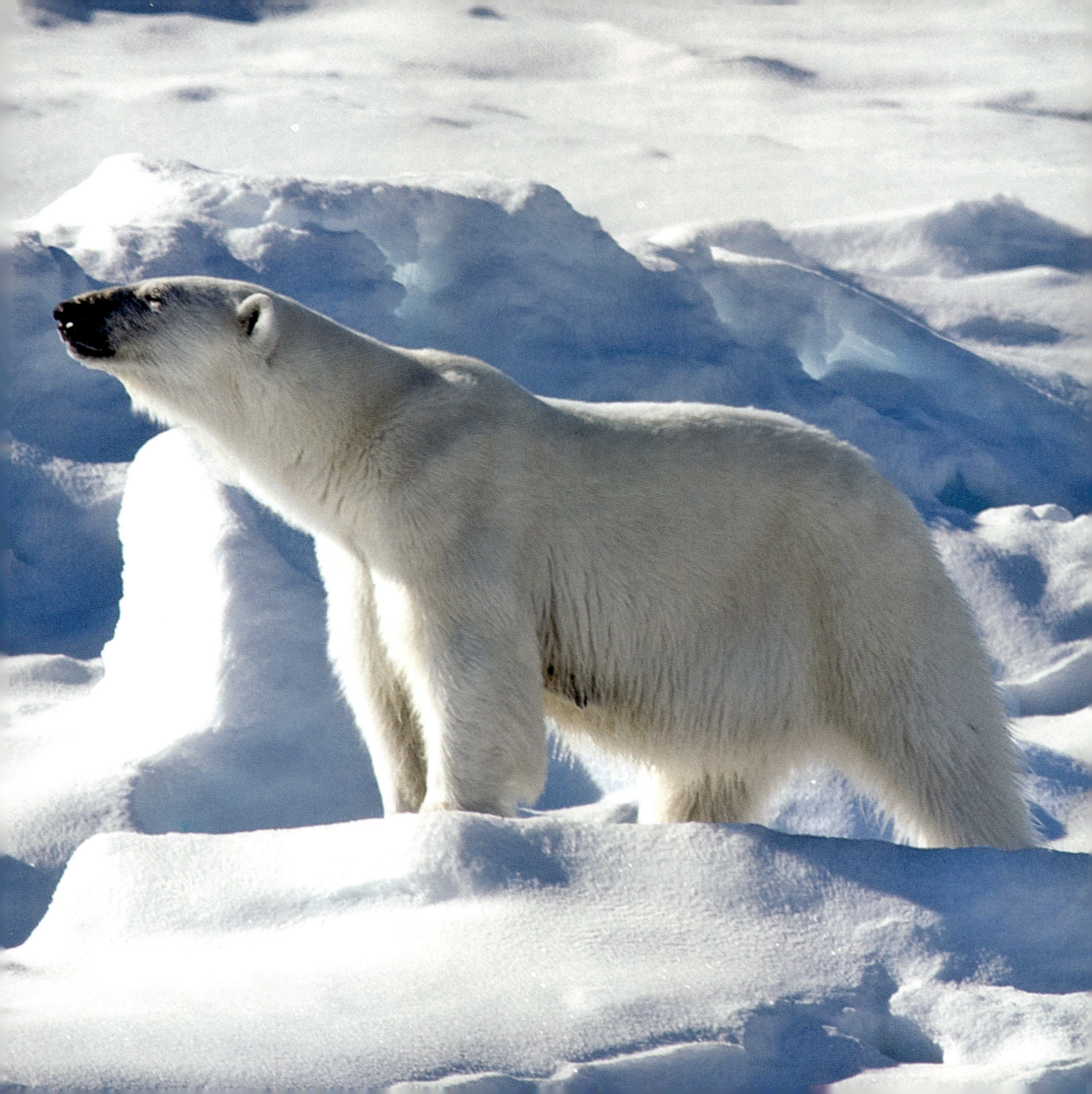

1. A Polar Bear's Meal
2. Hunting
3. Bears and Bears
4. A Bear's World
5. Habitat
6. The Polar Bear's Body
7. Built to Swim
8. Mommies and Cubs
9. The Polar Bear's Family
10. From Brown Bears to White Bears
11. Myths and Legends

Lions? Tigers? Crocodiles? They are mighty hunters, but the largest land carnivore on our planet is the exciting and beautiful polar bear. Strong as they are, polar bears are also caring parents, patient hunters, and, unexpectedly, fantastic swimmers.

Unlike his cousin the brown bear, you won't see a polar bear in the woods or the forest. Polar bears evolved and adapted to survive in the snow and ice, and made the Arctic Circle their home. They roam the Arctic Ocean and all the land and seas that cover this region.

In this book you will learn all about what makes polar bears such beautiful and majestic symbols of power, resilience, and beauty: you will learn about their size, weight, and strength; about their hunting abilities and habits; about their habitat, different species and family members; and many more interesting facts, in this Great Book About Polar Bears.

Of all bear family, from the little sun bear to the huge brown bear, the polar bear is the most carnivorous. In fact, polar bears are considered hypercarnivores, meaning their diet is more than 70% meat.

They mainly feed on bearded and ringed seals, but depending on where they live, they may also eat hooded and harp seals. Also, they can feed off the carcasses of walruses, beluga whales, bowhead whales, and narwhals.

Age plays an important role in what they eat too - while the young bears get the red meat (which is full of protein), older bears take the more calorific skin and blubber.

harp seal

ringed seal

A POLAR BEAR'S MEAL

What if there are no seals around? Well, a bear does have to eat, and so they've been known to go for seabirds, reindeer, fish, small rodents, waterfowl, berries, vegetation (such as kelp), and human garbage (that's right, our own waste!). Very hungry polar bears will even climb risky cliffs to get chicks and eggs from bird nests.

bearded seal

I need a bath!

DID YOU KNOW?

Polar bears rub themselves with water or snow to keep clean. After a meal, or sometimes during a meal, they will roll in the water or snow to clean their coat. This is important because a clean coat keeps them warm in the harsh and cold winds of the arctic.

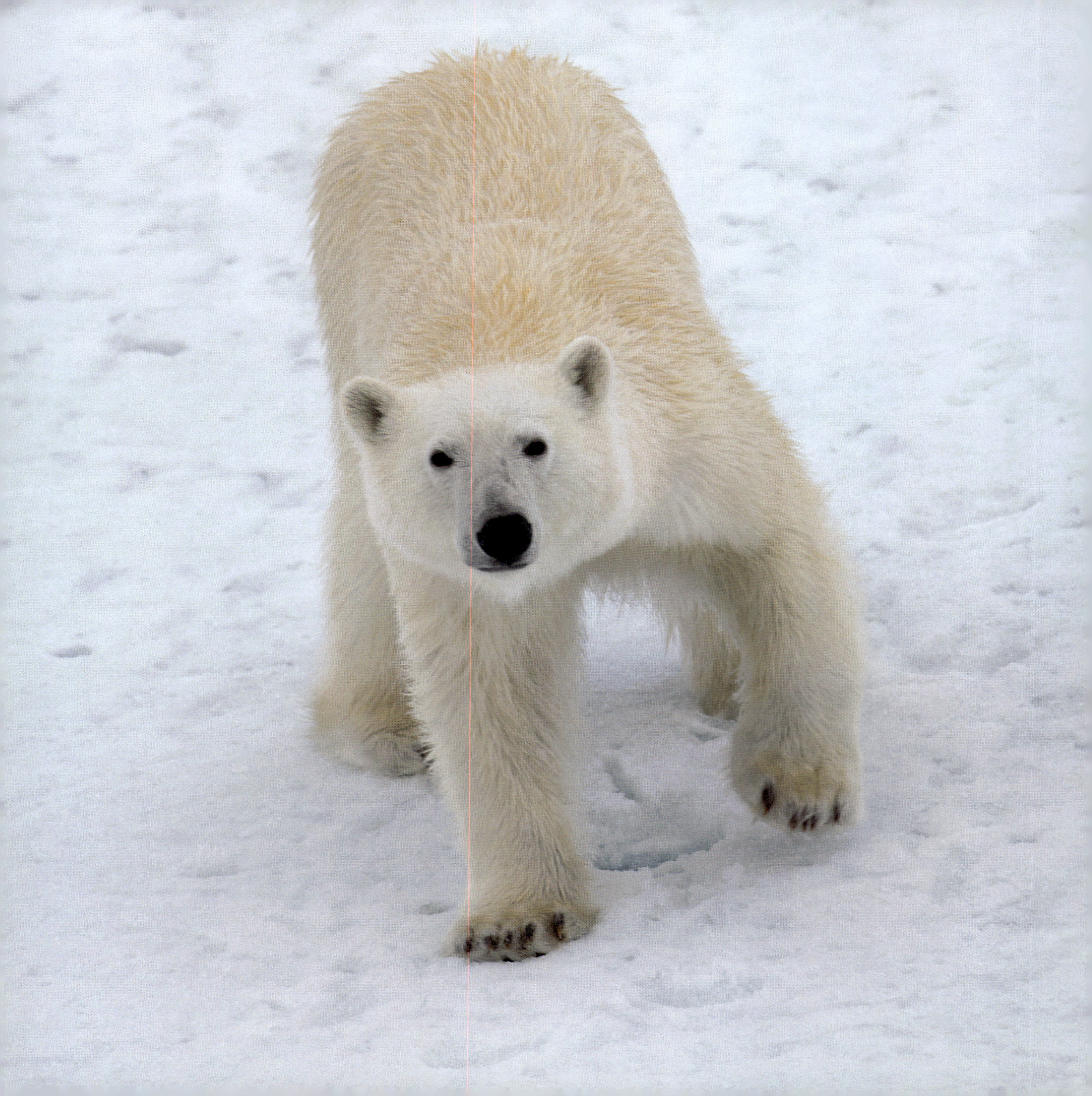

HUNTING

Looking for your next meal, in the cold and barren ice sheets of the arctic, is surely no easy task. But the white bear is an astute and skilled predator, always alert and ready to adapt its hunting methods to any situation that arises.

Polar bears are no fussy eaters, but seals are their go to food. When the bear detects a seal's breathing hole in an ice sheet, it will wait quietly and motionless for the seal to appear. Patience is key, as the waiting can take over an hour, and any sound or movement can spook the prey away. When the unsuspected seal finally pops out, the big bear will try to grab it with its claws or teeth, and flip it completely on to the ice.

Stalking is another hunting method employed by polar bears, when a seal is resting or warming up in the sun, out of water. Once spotted, the seal is slowly and silently stalked by the polar bear. At 15 to 30 m (49-98 ft.) away, the polar bear suddenly charges its prey, trying to grab it before the seal can leave the ice.

Because they are such good swimmers, polar bears also use the stalking method when hunting seal hauled out on sea ice. The bear will swim toward its target, quickly emerging from the water when close enough, to grab the seal tight with its claws or teeth.

In spring, polar bears sometimes stalk ringed seals at their birth lairs, caves built by the seal under snow drifts. The big bear slowly and quietly positions itself next to the lair, and if it smells or hears a seal in the lair, it slowly raises up on its hind legs and crashes down with its front paws to break through the lair's roof.

DID YOU KNOW?

Might and strong as polar bears are, life is not easy for them. Hunting is a difficult task, and usually polar bears only catch one or two out of ten seals they hunt. Good news for the seals, although not so good news for our hungry bears!

The life of a polar bears is mostly a solitary one. Usually they are only seen with others when a female has cubs or during mating season. Occasionally they might be seen together at a dump site or feeding off a large whale carcass. In the warmer months in Canada, they can also wait on land together, for the ice to return , sharing food and even play fighting each other.

After a successful hunt, polar bears usually firmly defend their catch from others. But they are not greedy, and if there is enough, they can peacefully share their catch with other bears.

Female polar bears, or sows, are loving and caring moms. They will groom their cubs, show affection, and protect them at all costs. Genetic testing has proven that some female polar bears can even adopt orphan cubs, keeping them safe and caring for them as if they were their own.

BEARS AND BEARS

Young cubs like to tackle their siblings and imitate their mother's hunting techniques. Play fight is great fun for them, but they're also learning and practicing how to hunt, getting ready for their adult lives.

DID YOU KNOW?

Polar bears use their noses for communication. As well as greeting with nose-to-nose contact, they will gently touch another bear's nose when asking for permission to share food.

No better image represents the arctic, than that of a lonesome polar bear walking on the endless white ice. But the big bears are much more than big predators.

They are a keystone species, meaning they have a huge impact on the natural environment around them, and all their ecosystem would be very different without them. In some way, polar bears regulate the numbers and types of species that exist in the Arctic.

Arctic foxes, for example, will often follow polar bears around during winter, feeding on their leftovers. Glaucous gulls also go through what they can off of a kill, once the bear is done.

Many scientists believe that polar bears and ringed seals have a very close relationship - while the over-population of ringed seals help to regulate polar bear density, the predator nature of polar bears regulates ringed seals density and their reproductive success.

A BEAR'S WORLD

DID YOU KNOW?

The polar bear has no natural predators, and this is called an 'apex predator'. Does this mean they can relax? Nope, they still need to be careful of brown bears because they tend to get the pick of good carcasses before polar bears. Orcas also provide some threat to polar bears, but our furry friends are normally quick enough to swim away or clever enough to steer clear of nearby orca pods.

Found all around the circumpolar Arctic, Polar bears are perfectly adapted to the cold environment of the north. Depending on the ice conditions, they will travel and migrate over land and through water at different times of the year. Sea ice is essential for polar bears because they need it to travel and hunt their favorite prey: seals.

Most won't go as far as the north pole, because food there is rare. The big white bears usually prefer to stay along the edge of the polar basin, where the conditions are right for hunting, thanks to the ice present along the continental shelf.

Polar bears can be found in Alaska (USA), Canada, Russia, Greenland (Denmark) and Svalbard (Norway). If heavy pack ice is present, they will travel to the Bering Sea and the Gulf of St Lawrence. Otherwise, they're most commonly found in Labrador, Newfoundland, and Norway. The most southern location you're likely to find polar bears is James Bay, Canada.

HABITAT

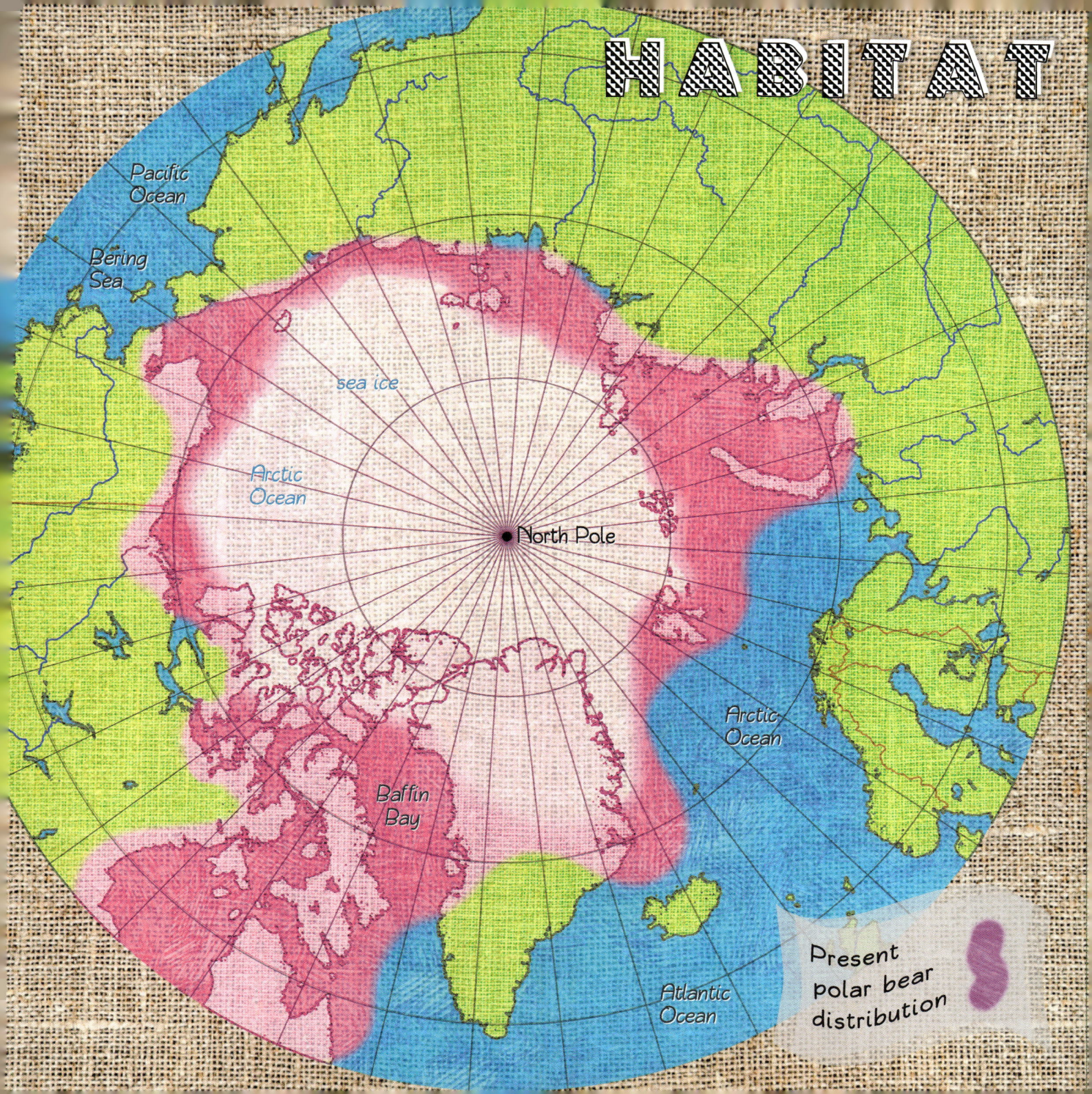

Brown bear or polar bear, who will take the title of the biggest land carnivore? And the winner is...the polar bear! It's a close one, but polar bears have longer heads and necks, and this is the secret to their victory.

Male bears, or boars, are usually at least twice as large as sows (the female bears), reaching between 2.5m and 3m long. Sows are between 1.8m to 2.5m, but still can weigh as much as 500kg, when pregnant.

The largest polar bear on record was 3.7m long and weighed an astonishing 1,000kg.

THE POLAR BEAR'S BODY

One very important feature of a polar bear is the nose, and this is because their acute sense of smell is key when hunting. According to experts, they can smell seals through 1 meter of snow and from over a kilometer away on land.

But that's not all: polar bears' nose are very sensible, and polar bears use them for communication. As well as greeting with nose-to-nose contact, they will gently touch another bear's nose when asking for permission to share food.

And how big are their paws? Tennis racket big, that's how! Up to 30cm in diameter. Like snowshoes for us humans, the pads carry the bear's weight and the partial webbing helps them to swim through the water.

Polar bears have black pads on their feet, with soft dermal bumps known as papillae. These bumps act as tire tracks, creating friction, and helping keep their grip on the slippery ice. Also, the toes have a thick, curved claw for grip when climbing and running, and to grab their prey while hunting.

Most polar bears will have a coat around 5cm thick, but there's actually two different types of hair. While the under layer is dense and woolly, there's a stiff and shiny layer of hair called 'guard hair' - these hairs can be as long as 15cm.

After swimming, they don't really have to worry about matting because of their oily, water-repellent fur. They can just shake off the water and carry on their day.

DID YOU KNOW?

The arctic is cold! Very cold! Water drops to a freezing 28.8°F (-1.8°C), and air temperatures reach -58 °F (-50 °C) during the winter. But this is not a problem for polar bears, because they are equipped with the ultimate extreme weather protection kit, including very dense fur, tough hide, and as much as 11cm of insulating fat layer. In fact, polar bears are so well isolated, they can even overheat. To avoid this, they stop and rest, slow down their pace, or go for an ice cold swim.

Polar bears are, most of all, amazing swimmers. They won't hesitate to get wet, crossing large portions of water, and reaching speeds of up to 10kph (6.2mph). A recent study tracked a sow swimming a record-breaking nine days straight, crossing 426 miles (687 kilometers) of water.

Polar bears are truly built to swim. Compared to other bears, their bodies have a more streamlined shape, with smaller shoulders, a large rump, and long, slender necks and heads. This helps them to slide through the cold arctic water, easily keeping their head above the surface.

BUILT TO SWIM

While swimming, polar bears rely on their front legs to move through water, using their hind legs as rudders, to change direction. They can also close their nostrils while submerged.

Polar bears tend to swim close to the surface, but they are also great divers. They use this skill to sneak up on their prey or to look for kelp. Most dives are not that long, but a polar bear was observed covering around 50 meters (160 feet) while staying underwater for over three minutes.

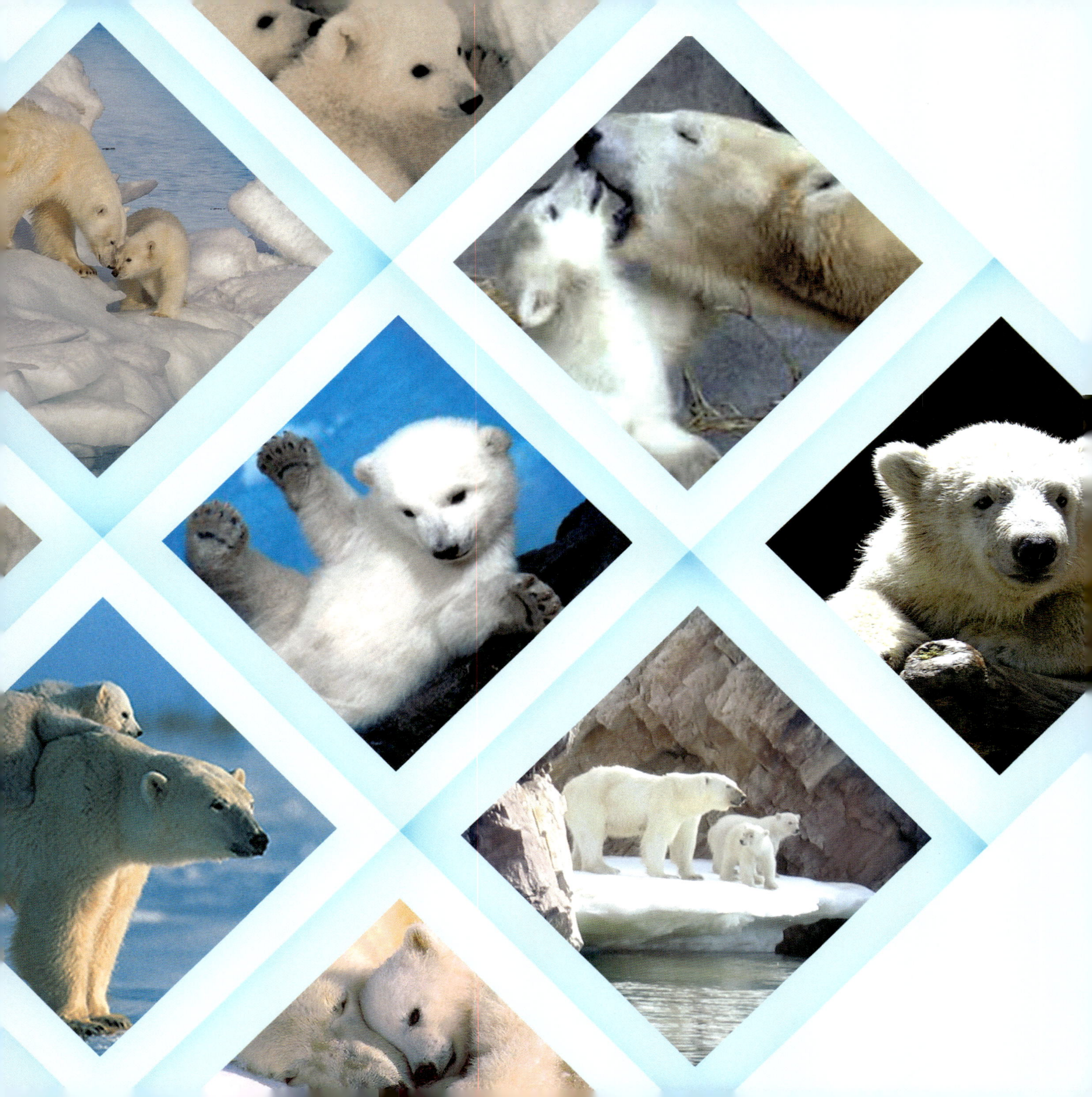

MOMMIES AND CUBS

Although dad bear doesn't have a role in raising their sons, with mom is a totally different story: Polar bear sows are amazing mothers, caring and ever watchful, even willing to risk their lives to protect their babies.

Cubs are born between November and January, in a den dug into a snowdrift. Polar bears usually give birth to two small cubs, weighing as little as 450 grams. They are born with thin fur and defenseless, totally depending on mom for warmth and food.

But the little balls of fur grow up fast, and after a couple of months they are big enough, and strong enough to venture outside. They now height around 15 kg, and are very active and curious, eager to explore the outside world.

Mom guides them to the sea ice, always watchful, even carrying them on her back in deep snow or water. Through watching their mother, the young ones learn to hunt, and by the age of two are already able to actively participate in the hunt.

It takes 30 months for the cubs to say goodbye, and this is when the mother will breed again. Sometimes a male chases the cubs away, and sometimes the male will notice the lack of cubs and start following the female, and the cycle repeats.

GIANT PANDA

ASIATIC BLACK BEAR

SUN BEAR

BROWN BEAR

The polar bear (Ursus maritimus) is the largest member of the bear (or Ursidae) family. Among others, this family also includes brown and black bears, sun bears, and the giant panda.

The oldest polar bear fossil to be found dates back around 130,000 years. With brown bears as an ancestor, the two bears are closely related.

SPECTACLED BEAR

AMERICAN BLACK BEAR

SLOTH BEAR

THE POLAR BEAR'S FAMILY

Polar bears are specially adapted for the cold temperatures, and for moving across snow, ice and open water of the Arctic.

Their scientific name, Ursus maritimus, actually means "maritime bear" - they are also considered marine mammals because they fully depend on the ocean for food and habitat.

Once upon a time, a long long time ago, a mighty brown bear roamed the cold lands of Eurasia. Our planet was a different place, back then. Cold was ever present, and ice covered most of North America, Asia and Europe.

The great bear, a beautiful sow, was in many ways just like any other of her kin: dark furred, powerful and intelligent. But, deep inside her, something extraordinary was happening...

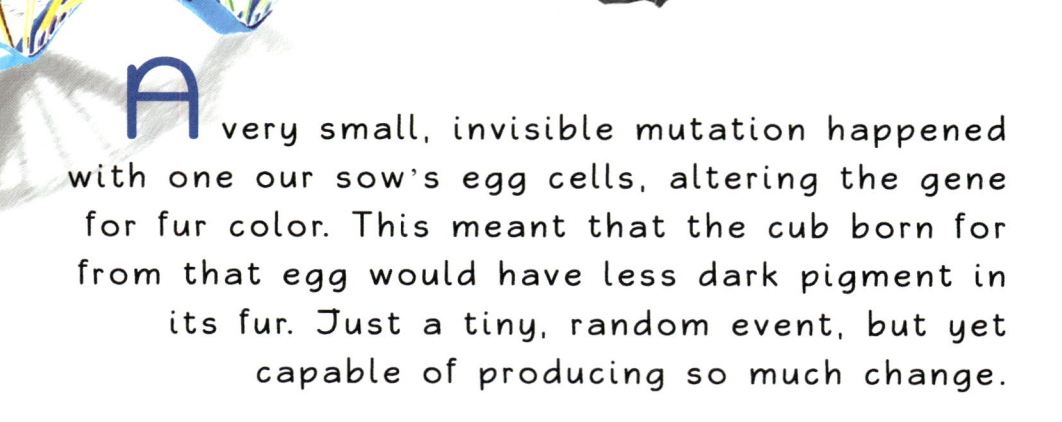

A very small, invisible mutation happened with one our sow's egg cells, altering the gene for fur color. This meant that the cub born for from that egg would have less dark pigment in its fur. Just a tiny, random event, but yet capable of producing so much change.

FROM BROWN BEARS TO WHITE BEARS

Time passed, and our mighty bear was now a proud and caring mother of two cubs. One just like her, with a beautiful dark coat, but another one very special: a white furred cub.

Some months later, the cubs where now old enough to venture hunting on their own, and soon their differences became clear.

While the dark furred cub could be easily spotted in the white ice and snow, from far away, the white one could get much closer to its prey without being exposed.

So the white bear grew big and strong, passing along its white fur gene to its offspring, who too thrived in these hard conditions. Generation after generation, the white fur gene spread, to the entire population of arctic bears.

Over time, the two bear populations separated. The darker bears where still at home in the southern forests and woodlands, but now the white bears ruled the vast ice and snow fields of the north.

Over thousands of years, they also developed other features that set them apart, like teeth adapted to hunt seals, thicker insulation to better handle the cold weather, and wider semi-webbed paws to aid swimming and walking on ice and snow.

They became a different species – the polar bear.

DID YOU KNOW?

This is what is called "evolution by natural selection", a concept first presented by Charles Darwin in 1859, in his revolutionary book "On the Origin of Species".

Since long ago, the mighty white bear has been a source of inspiration for those living among them. Their raw power, but also their nobility and serenity grant them a mystical, almost magical aura, leaving no one indifferent.

Inuit carved antler, depicting a seated polar bear

The polar bear's human-like posture when sitting down or standing, has led to a spiritual and physical connection between man and beast. Local folks talk of a star constellation of a bear surrounded by dogs, and others even believe the bears are actually humans in a bear hide.

8¢ polar bear and cubs stamp

To the Inuit, Nanuk was the master of all bears, for whom they had great respect. He was powerful and strong, and the Inuit hunters would ask for his help and guidance, for they believed he would decide if the hunt would be a successful one.

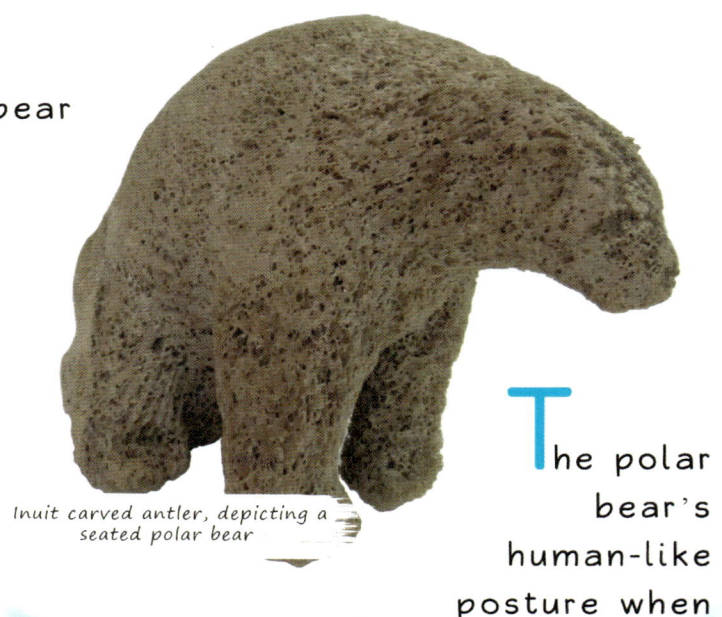

Inuit carved scene with a polar bear and a seal

MYTHS AND LEGENDS

The Chukchi and Yupik people, of eastern Siberia, would appease the spirit of the hunted bear by playing traditional songs and drum music, as a thank you for its sacrifice. Another community in Siberia, the Nenets, would see great power in the polar bears' huge canine teeth. They believed sewing the teeth into their hat would offer protection from the dangerous brown bears.

Among all the legends and stories, one thing is clear; polar bears have always had great respect from humans. We should do our best to ensure a bright future for these wonderful animals.

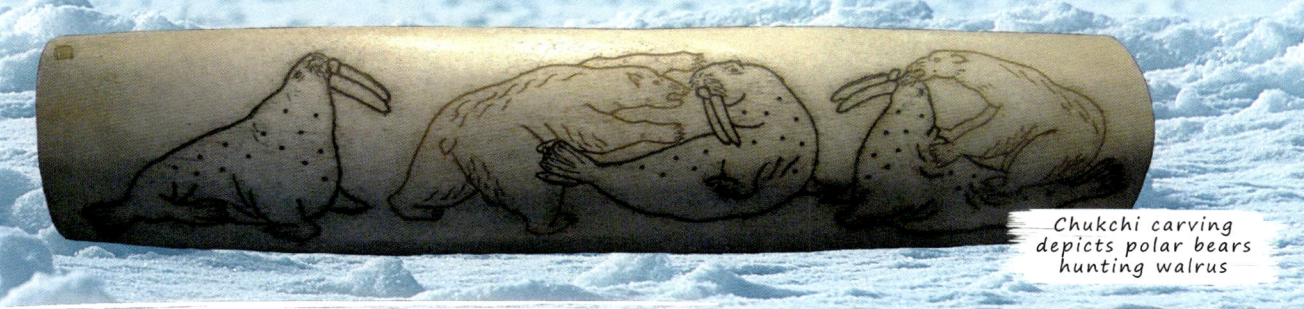

Chukchi carving depicts polar bears hunting walrus

DID YOU KNOW?

Some say that people in the Arctic gained igloo construction and seal hunting skills from polar bears. Essentially, polar bear dens and igloos have a similar construction because it's all about trapping warm air inside ice and snow (while still bringing in fresh air through a ventilation hole).

Photo Credits

Cover – 358611/Pixabay
Front Page – A. Weith/Wikipedia
A Word from the Author – Christopher Michel/Flickr
Index – Christopher Michel/Flickr
A Polar Bear's Meal – Wasif Malik/Flickr; Andreas Weith/Wikipedia; kerryinlondon/Flickr; Kingfisher/Wikipedia; Virginia State Parks/Flickr
Hunting – Christopher Michel/Flickr
Hunting (2nd Page) – Dennis Larsen/Pixabay; Emma/Flickr
Bears and Bears – MF /Wikimedia; Vasilyev Serge/Flickr; US Fish and Wildlife Service/Flickr; Anita Ritenour/Flickr; Lorie Shaull/Flickr
A Bear's World – Christopher Michel/Flickr;
The Polar Bear's Body – Christopher Michel/Flickr
The Polar Bear's Body (2nd Page) – Gerd Altmann/Pixabay; PublicDomainPictures/Pixabay; Tambako The Jaguar/Flickr; Tambako The Jaguar/Flickr; Dick Hoskins/Pexels
Built to Swim – Christopher Michel/Flickr; Anita Ritenour/Flickr; Brian Gratwicke/Flickr; Helene Berger/Pixabay; John/Flickr
Mommies and Cubs – Alastair Rae/Flickr; beingmyself/Flickr; Andrea Bohl/Pixabay; Andreas Weith/Wikimedia
The Polar Bear's Family – beingmyself/Flickr; 358611/Pixabay; user_272447/Pixabay; Tambako the Jaguar/Flickr; Diginatur/Wikipedia; Andreas Marz/Flickr; 995645/Pixabay; Art G/Flickr; BSBCC/Wikimedia
From Brown Bears to White Bears – National Human Genome Research Institute/Flickr; Pierfilippo Mancini/Flickr; tambako the jaguar/Flickr; tambako the jaguar/Flickr; Alan D. Wilson/Nature's Pics Online
From Brown Bears to White Bears (2nd Page) – tambako the jaguar/Flickr; Hans-Jurgen Mager/Unsplash
Myths and Legends – Christopher Michel/Flickr; Wildlife Conservation/Wikimedia; Brooklyn Museum/ Brooklyn Museum; Eliezg/Wikimedia
Credits – Karilop311/Flickr

THE GREAT BOOK ABOUT POLAR BEARS ©2021 ALL RIGHTS RESERVED.
ISBN: 9798530412776

QWERTY BOOKS

Printed in Great Britain
by Amazon